AF379989

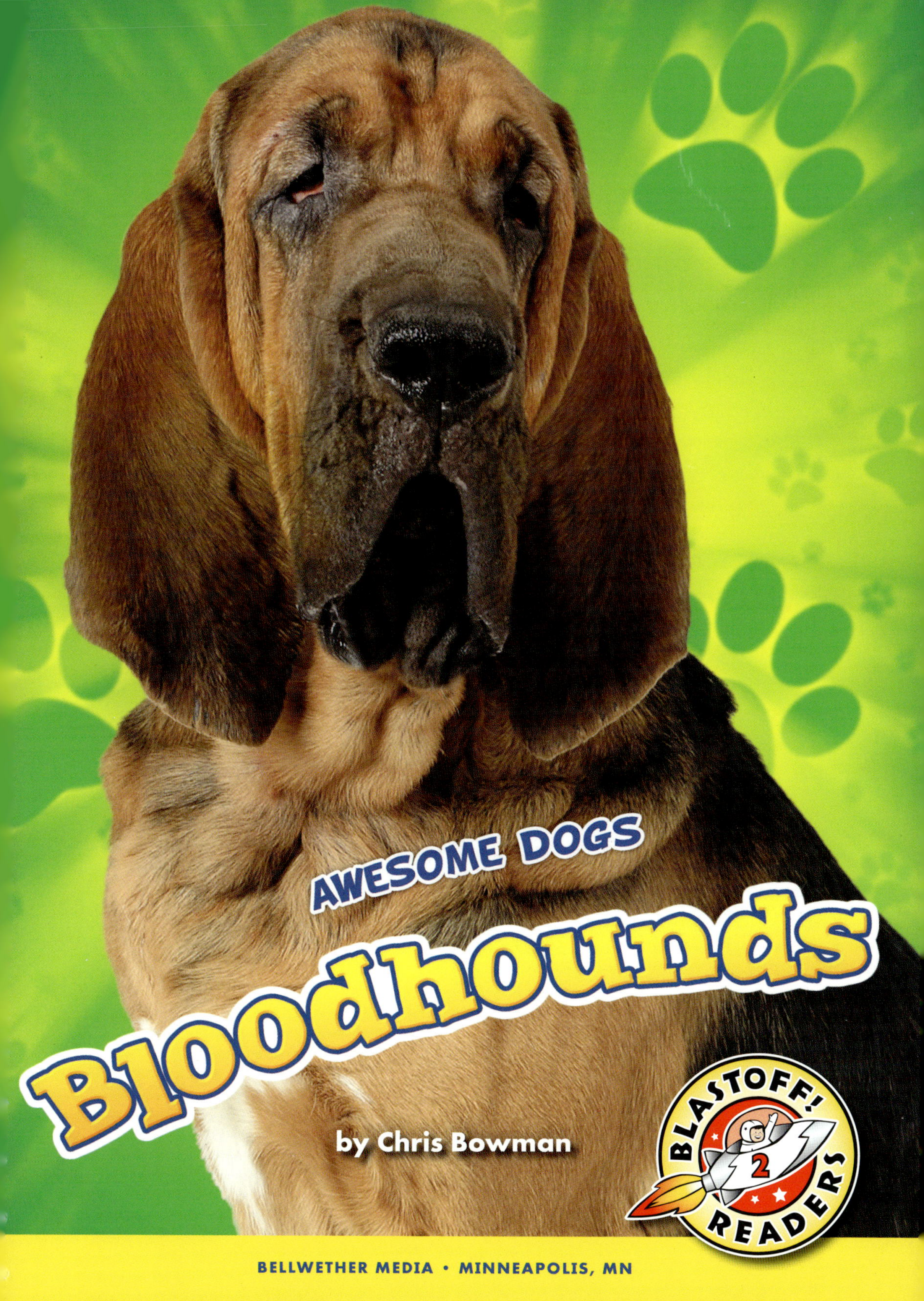

AWESOME DOGS
Bloodhounds
by Chris Bowman
BLASTOFF! READERS
2
BELLWETHER MEDIA • MINNEAPOLIS, MN

Note to Librarians, Teachers, and Parents:

Blastoff! Readers are carefully developed by literacy experts and combine standards-based content with developmentally appropriate text.

Level 1 provides the most support through repetition of high-frequency words, light text, predictable sentence patterns, and strong visual support.

Level 2 offers early readers a bit more challenge through varied simple sentences, increased text load, and less repetition of high-frequency words.

Level 3 advances early-fluent readers toward fluency through increased text and concept load, less reliance on visuals, longer sentences, and more literary language.

Level 4 builds reading stamina by providing more text per page, increased use of punctuation, greater variation in sentence patterns, and increasingly challenging vocabulary.

Level 5 encourages children to move from "learning to read" to "reading to learn" by providing even more text, varied writing styles, and less familiar topics.

Whichever book is right for your reader, Blastoff! Readers are the perfect books to build confidence and encourage a love of reading that will last a lifetime!

This edition first published in 2020 by Bellwether Media, Inc.

Library of Congress Cataloging-in-Publication Data

Names: Bowman, Chris, 1990- author.
Title: Bloodhounds / by Chris Bowman.
Description: Minneapolis, MN : Bellwether Media, Inc., [2020] | Series:
   Blastoff! Readers: Awesome Dogs | Audience: Age 5-8. | Audience: K to
   Grade 3. | Includes bibliographical references and index.
Identifiers: LCCN 2018057359 (print) | LCCN 2018058644 (ebook) | ISBN
   9781618915467 (ebook) | ISBN 9781644870051 (hardcover : alk. paper)
Subjects: LCSH: Bloodhound–Juvenile literature.
Classification: LCC SF429.B6 (ebook) | LCC SF429.B6 B69 2020 (print) | DDC 636.753/6–dc23
LC record available at https://lccn.loc.gov/2018057359

Editor: Al Albertson   Designer: Laura Sowers

Printed in the United States of America, North Mankato, MN.

Table of Contents

Bloodhounds are **curious** and friendly dogs. They are sometimes called Saint Hubert hounds.

Bloodhounds have a strong sense of smell. They are known to drool a lot!

Bloodhounds have long
and **wrinkly** faces.
Their eyes sit deep
in the folds of their skin.

Big ears droop down
the sides of their heads.

Bloodhounds have big and strong bodies. They usually weigh around 100 pounds (45 kilograms)!

Their necks often have
loose skin that hangs down.

9

Bloodhounds have short **coats**. Some coats are **liver** and tan.

Others are black and tan.
Bloodhounds can even be red!

Dogs similar to bloodhounds have been around for thousands of years.

The earliest bloodhounds came from **medieval** Western Europe.

Early bloodhounds were **noble** dogs. They were **bred** by **Catholic monks**.

They helped hunt boar
and deer. Some tracked
down people.

Over time, these prized dogs spread throughout the world.

Today, the **American Kennel Club** places them in the **Hound Group**.

Many bloodhounds work in **search and rescue**. Their sense of smell also helps police.

Bloodhounds follow their noses. They will not stop until they find what they are looking for!

Bloodhounds are **pack** dogs.
They like to go for walks with
people and other dogs.

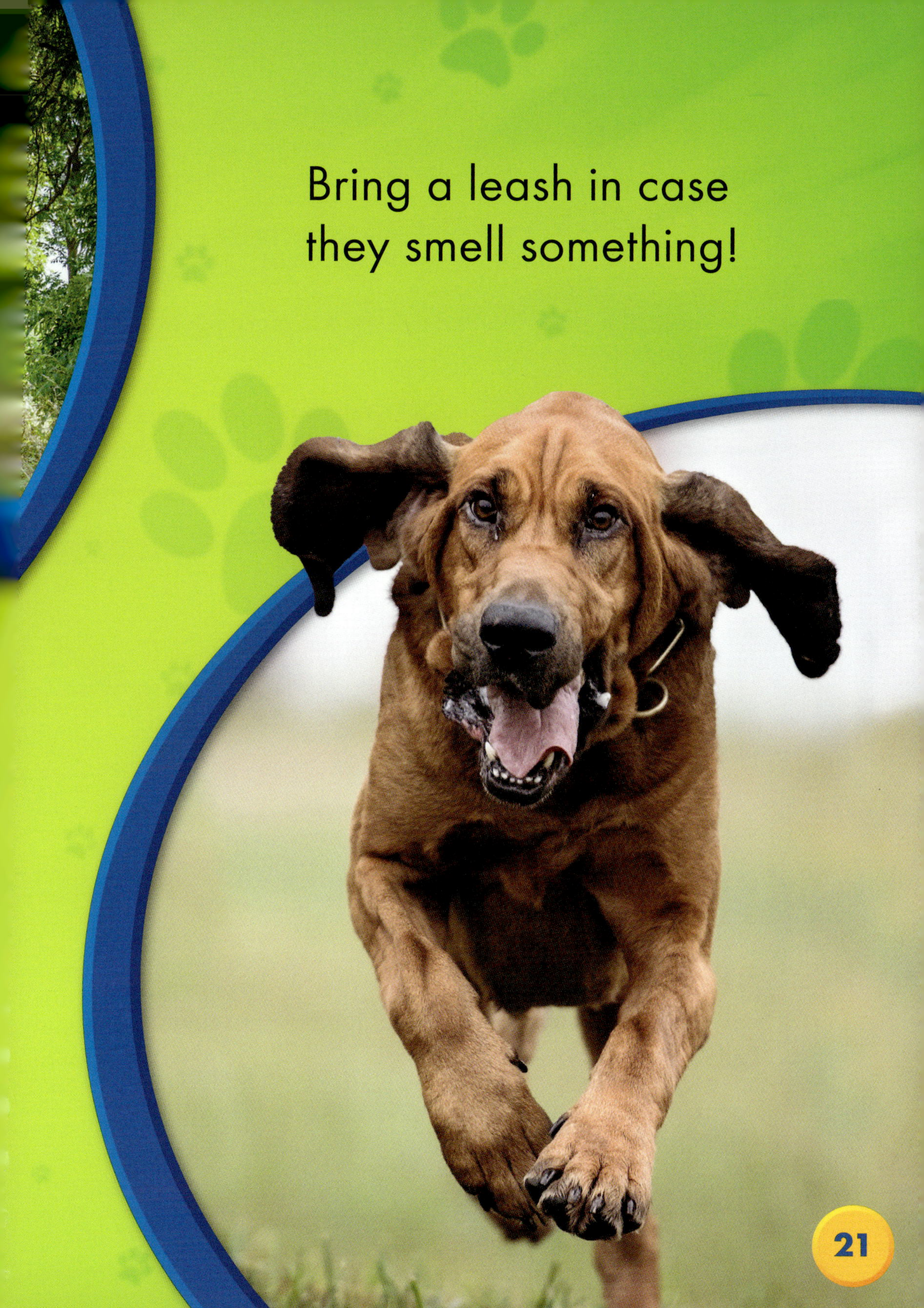

Bring a leash in case
they smell something!

Glossary

American Kennel Club—an organization that keeps track of dog breeds in the United States

bred—purposely mated two dogs to make puppies with certain qualities

Catholic monks—men who follow the Catholic religion and live apart from other people; monks have many rules that they must follow.

coats—the hair or fur covering some animals

curious—interested or excited to learn or know about something

Hound Group—a group of dog breeds that often have a history of hunting

liver—brown

medieval—from the Middle Ages

noble—related to the upper class

pack—a group that lives together

search and rescue—teams that look and care for people in danger

wrinkly—full of lines in the skin or fur

To Learn More

AT THE LIBRARY

Gagne, Tammy. *The Dog Encyclopedia for Kids.* North Mankato, Minn.: Capstone Young Readers, 2017.

Polinsky, Paige V. *Basset Hounds.* Minneapolis, Minn.: Bellwether Media, 2018.

Schuh, Mari. *Beagles.* Minneapolis, Minn.: Bellwether Media, 2016.

ON THE WEB

FACTSURFER

Factsurfer.com gives you a safe, fun way to find more information.

1. Go to www.factsurfer.com.

2. Enter "bloodhounds" into the search box and click 🔍.

3. Select your book cover to see a list of related web sites.

Index

The images in this book are reproduced through the courtesy of: Kuznetsov Alexey, cover, pp. 11 (middle), 14; Lenkada, pp. 4-5, 16; adogslifephoto, p. 5; Degtyaryov Andrey, pp. 6-7; Edoma, pp. 7, 10-11; Farlap/ Alamy, pp. 8-9; jadimages, p. 9; Erik Lam, p. 11 (left); Susan Schmitz, p. 11 (right); Marzolino, pp. 12, 14-15; Helen Sushitskaya, p. 13; CaptureLight, p. 17; NSC Photography, pp. 18-19, 21; dpa picture alliance/ Alamy, p. 19; Matt Limb OBE/ Alamy, pp. 20-21.